Festive Spirits

Three Short Stories

www.penguin.co.uk

Also by Kate Atkinson

Behind the Scenes at the Museum
Human Croquet
Emotionally Weird
Not the End of the World
Life After Life
A God in Ruins
Transcription

FEATURING JACKSON BRODIE

Case Histories
One Good Turn
When Will There Be Good News?
Started Early, Took My Dog
Big Sky

Festive Spirits

Three Short Stories

Kate Atkinson

doubleday

TRANSWORLD PUBLISHERS
61–63 Uxbridge Road, London W5 5SA
www.penguin.co.uk

Transworld is part of the Penguin Random House group of companies
whose addresses can be found at global.penguinrandomhouse.com

Penguin
Random House
UK

'Lucy's Day' first published in *Good Housekeeping*;
'Festive Spirit' first published by the *New Statesman*
This collection first published in Great Britain in 2019 by Doubleday
an imprint of Transworld Publishers

A CIP catalogue record for this book
is available from the British Library.

ISBN 9780857527127

Typeset in 13.5/18.5pt Garamond MT Std by Jouve (UK), Milton Keynes
Printed and bound in Great Britain by Clays Ltd, Elcograf S.p.A.

Penguin Random House is committed to a sustainable
future for our business, our readers and our planet. This book
is made from Forest Stewardship Council® certified paper.

MIX
Paper from
responsible sources
FSC
www.fsc.org   FSC® C018179

3 5 7 9 10 8 6 4 2

Contents

Lucy's Day

Lucy liked the new one best. The other three were practice pieces towards the perfection of the fourth. Ben. Three months old and counting. Much the nicest so far, 'Don't you think?' Lucy said. Stephen looked up from the book he was reading and, glancing briefly at his wife and guzzling baby lying next to him in bed, said, 'Yeah, I like that one.'

'Me too.'

The other three – Beatrice, Maude and Millie – had been furious babies, red-faced, clutching their fists like tiny boxers, bellowing their way through the dark watches of the night. They hadn't improved much since, whereas Ben was placid, contented, almost stupefied.

'He's all right, isn't he?' Stephen said. 'You don't think there's something wrong with him?'

'No, I just think this is what a good baby looks like. Who knew?'

'You can probably stop having them now that we've got a keeper.'

'You're right,' Lucy said. 'We've done our bit towards providing fodder for the capitalist system. Although can I just point out that while, technically speaking, it was me that *had* them, it takes two to *make* them. According to the birds and bees anyway.'

'Well, I'm certainly not about to contradict the birds and bees,' Stephen said. 'They can be very argumentative.' He removed his glasses and rolled towards her.

'Watch out, you'll squash the baby,' Lucy said.

'It's OK, we can get another.'

'Aw, the baby Jesus,' Pearl said. 'Inteelovely?' Pearl was sixty-five years old but could have passed for a hundred. She had a hacking cough ('Milungs'), a curiously bent leg, and was beset by grown-up, warring offspring ('Our Dean', 'Our Grant' and the notoriously free-spirited 'Our Lesley'). Pearl had arrived in their lives after Beatrice's birth as a temporary measure and had never gone away.

'Nothing like the Christmas story, is there?' Pearl said.

'Well . . .' Lucy said, glancing down doubtfully at the misshapen piece of pink plasticine masquerading as the new Messiah in the Nativity scene that Beatrice had brought home from school the previous day. Lucy was on a ladder, hanging swags of ivy salvaged from the wasteland at the bottom of the garden. She was making the most of the fact that both Millie and Ben were asleep. Their naps coincided only once in a thousand years.

The Nativity was a dishevelled construct made mostly, as far as Lucy could tell, from lollipop sticks, cotton wool and hamster-bedding. And lentils. The school used lentils a lot in its artwork, as well as pasta and beans. You could have made soup from some of the collages Beatrice and Maude brought home. Lucy would have liked to protest on behalf of all the starving people in the world but she was worried her children would be punished, subjected to some kind of excommunication. Millie was only three but Beatrice and Maude went to a Church of England school that you had to fight tooth and nail to get into. One day, inevitably, someone would be murdered to secure a place for a little Harry or an Emily, all so they could sing hymns to the baby Jesus every morning and wear a ridiculously pompous uniform.

Lucy believed in state education but the local primary was struggling – overcrowded and underfunded. They had considered a private school and Lucy worried about just how far they were prepared to go to compromise their ethics on behalf of their children. 'All the way,' Stephen said. In the end they settled on St Martin's, the C of E school near by. They (the parents, not the children) had to go through all kinds of hoops to get in. Three interviews before being accepted, including one, finally, in their own home, for which Pearl had done a double shift to make the house look slightly less of a child-infested shambles for the visit of the headmistress, a woman called Harriet Raven who was so neat and tidy she looked as if she had just come fresh out of a box.

'Babies, eh?' Pearl said, looking at a sleeping Ben. 'I could eat him.'

'Oh, please don't,' Lucy said.

They couldn't really afford Pearl any more, but they were the only people she cleaned for these days and if she lost their money she wouldn't have anything. She didn't really clean, she just limped around and shook a duster at things. As if it wasn't enough that Lucy had the trees and the bees and the melting ice-caps to worry about, she also had to put Pearl on her list of endangered species.

'If only we could hide the girls,' Lucy said to Stephen before the advent of Harriet Raven, 'put them in a cupboard or something so she can't see what savages they are.'

'She'll probably look in the cupboards.' (She did!)

Harriet Raven came with a small posse of Inquisitors. Both Lucy and Stephen lied outrageously under the torture of having to sip tea and nibble on shortbread in the company of people seemingly intent on finding them unfit. ('We are unfit,' Stephen pointed out.) Yes, they certainly did believe in God, in the monarchy, in early bedtimes; no, they didn't believe in sweets, in television, in swearing. When their examiners had finally gone, Lucy fell on to the sofa and said, 'Christ on a bike, that was hard,' before turning on *The Real Housewives of Orange County* and working her way through a giant packet of Maltesers.

Lucy had given up work to stay at home

after Millie was born. Now, she couldn't imagine why she thought that had been a good idea. She'd been a barrister, arguing criminal defence cases in the High Court. These days she spent her time wrangling a pack of feral girls, for which you needed the skills of a surgeon and the nerve of a rodeo rider. To take only yesterday as an example, she had untangled the gerbil from Beatrice's hair and extricated Millie from the dog flap, where she had become stuck half in, half out (to the dog's surprise). All of this had been trumped by Maude jumping off the shed roof and ending up in A & E with a greenstick fracture to her arm. 'But Father Christmas can fly,' she wailed. 'Why can't I?' 'Because you don't have any reindeer,' Lucy said reasonably. The High Court had been infinitely less challenging.

They had overindulged, she thought.

Four was an excessive number. Global warming, poverty, all Four Horsemen of the Apocalypse galloping her way were all good arguments against over-reproduction. But Lucy liked to imagine that when she was old one of the compensations would be the bountiful, not to mention grateful, generations gathered around her skirts. (Stephen didn't figure in this future – statistically speaking he would be dead.) Of course, if those same generations were as rabid as Beatrice, Maude and Millie they would probably eat her alive.

She feared death, she feared time's winged chariot, but the idea that her genes would sail into the future, keeping a tiny part of her alive for ever, made mortality seem less awful to Lucy. The heart may die but the DNA goes on.

'Existential angst,' Stephen said. 'Now

that God is dead you need something to believe in. You've opted for babies. I personally put faith in the idea that one day I'll own a Maserati GranTurismo. It's not heaven, but it's pretty close.'

The vicar of St Martin's had been one of Harriet Raven's fellow Inquisitors. Like Harriet she was a woman of many astonishing certainties and spoke a lot about heaven in her services. It seemed an unlikely place to Lucy, full of romping dogs and loving relatives waiting to welcome you with open arms. Lucy imagined her mother, dead last year, casting a cold eye on her as she approached the pearly gates, saying, 'Goodness, Lucy, what on earth are you wearing?'

Lucy always skulked at the back of the church; it was like being at school again, trying not to make eye contact with the insanely cheerful vicar. Part of the pact they had made with the devil (or Harriet Raven, as she was also known) was that not only were they regular churchgoers but they would continue to be so. Lies compounded by lies. Stephen had gone to St Martin's a couple of times for show but couldn't be persuaded any more. 'Claptrap' was his verdict on religion. At least the children were happy to be herded into Sunday school, where they listened enthusiastically to stories of unlikely miracles and produced yet more collages based on soup ingredients.

Lucy, born and bred an atheist, regarded herself as, if anything, a kind of animist, believing that the spirit of nature lived in the trees and the hills and the rivers. She would have felt more comfortable worshipping a rock than the Holy Trinity, but when Harriet Raven asked, 'Are you a churchgoer?' Lucy didn't say, 'Well, actually I'm a bit of a heathen,' and instead said, 'Absolutely. Regular as clockwork,' so that now she found herself sitting every Sunday amongst the dying embers of a congregation, mouthing the words to hymns and prayers. It wasn't so bad – actually it was quite good as she spent most of the time making mental shopping-lists or practising deep breathing. Sometimes she just sat and enjoyed the peace.

'You're much better at commitment than I am,' Stephen said.

'Am I?' Lucy said. Stephen was very handsome. That was the thing that had attracted Lucy to him (no point in being dishonest at this juncture in their marriage). He had a lovely voice – deep, sexy, posh but not offensively so. His parents ran a gift shop in Margate and were constantly startled by the good-looking, polished son they had produced. He would have made an excellent politician: he had good hair and lied easily. If Lucy had had time between nappies and feeds and school runs, she would have worried that he was having affairs.

'Don't be silly,' he said. 'I'm too exhausted.'

'The right answer is that you love me and would never be unfaithful to me.'

'That too.'

'Never marry a handsome man,' Lucy said to Pearl.

'I'll try not to,' Pearl said.

Stephen had a meeting he couldn't get out of and was not able to attend the end-of-term Nativity play. 'Don't think I wouldn't rather,' he said. He was halfway to the car before he realized he still had a sleeping Ben draped like a tea-towel on his shoulder.

15

'You're planning to run away and take the good one with you,' Lucy accused him.

'You've got me bang to rights, lady,' he said, handing the baby back.

Lucy took Pearl to the school instead.

'Lovely,' Pearl said as they sat on hard, uncomfortable chairs in a school gymnasium that was festooned with gaudy Christmas decorations that looked like fire hazards. Millie crawled underneath Pearl's chair because she was pretending to be a dog.

'Don't bite my ankles,' Pearl said.

'She might,' Lucy said.

'I know.'

'Did you know that today's St Lucy's Day?' Lucy said to Pearl.

'Your day!'

'Yes, I suppose it is. St Lucy's Day used to be on the midwinter solstice before they changed the calendar.'

'They changed the calendar?' Pearl asked, looking alarmed.

'Hundreds of years ago.'

'Men, I'll bet,' Pearl tutted.

'*The day's deep midnight*, John Donne calls St Lucy's.'

'Does he now?' Pearl said.

'I think St Lucy was a pagan goddess before the Church took her over. They nabbed all the best festivals. Lucy means light. That's what midwinter festivals are all about, the return of the light to the world.'

'That's nice. Have a Revel.'

Maude, arm in a cast, was the smallest sheep in a restless, badly behaved flock that was in dire need of a sheepdog. A scowling Beatrice was one of the heavenly host – a large cast of extras who shuffled their feet and picked their noses at the back.

'I predict a riot,' Lucy murmured.

'Our Lesley was an angel once,' Pearl said.

'Really?' Lucy said. It was hard to imagine.

Would her children be happy? Lucy wondered. Probably not. Hardly anyone was. Little moments – that was the best you could ask for, an epiphany here and there, the occasional short-lived burst of joy. The world turning one more time. The sun coming up, the spring returning, a baby waking up and smiling at you. Little lights in the dark.

Harriet Raven clapped her hands to signal the start. The Angel Gabriel walked warily on stage and the parental iPhones were held aloft in worship.

'Lo and behold,' Lucy said.

'Aw,' Pearl said appreciatively, as the shepherds and their unruly flock made their

18

appearance and gathered round the baby Jesus. Until yesterday he had been a Tiny Tears doll but now he was Ben, dragooned into playing the starring role. He lay peacefully asleep in a slightly too-small cradle so that he looked like a fat happy pea alone in its pod.

'Inteegood?' Pearl said appreciatively.

'He is,' Lucy said.

Lucy would have challenged anyone not to cry at the sight of their child in a Nativity play. Even a sheepish Maude, even a scowling Beatrice — currently attempting a Chinese burn on an adjacent angel.

Pearl was singing along to 'Away In A Manger' like a Nativity veteran.

A shepherd shouted something incomprehensible to Joseph. One of the Wise Men wet himself. Beatrice waved enthusiastically, a little too enthusiastically, at Lucy from the angelic choir. It was better than any religion, Lucy thought.

'Awright?' Pearl asked.

'I'm having an epiphany.'

'Sounds painful.'

'Not at all,' Lucy laughed. 'Although I expect I'll pay for it later. That's generally the way of things.'

'Isn't it just? Enjoy it while you can.'

Pearl of Wisdom, Lucy thought. 'Happy Christmas, Pearl.'

'Happy Christmas, Lucy.'

Festive Spirit

'Here's to you, Sal,' he said loudly, chinking his glass with hers so that the wine within sloshed around carelessly. 'Happy birthday.' He glanced around the restaurant, feigning amused tolerance for his surroundings. It was Lebanese, in Camden. It irritated him that no one seemed to know who he was here. He liked to bask in recognition, even if it was hostile.

The world's resources of tinsel had been seriously depleted in order to decorate the restaurant. 'A bit tacky, isn't it?' Richard said with a little shudder. 'Wouldn't it be better,' he'd grumbled, when she told him where they were going, 'if I was seen flying the flag? Somewhere more British. English, anyway – the Scots dine on lard and I don't think the Welsh have restaurants.' A lot of people seemed to find this kind of blustering talk amusing, thinking that he didn't really mean it, that he was some kind of clown to be tolerated, treasured even, in some quarters. 'I mean,' he dropped his voice, 'they're Muslims. They don't even celebrate Christmas, for heaven's sake.'

'Well, forty per cent of Lebanese are Christian,' she pointed out. 'Just as well you've never been in the Foreign Office.'

'Hah.'

'You said I could choose the restaurant,' Sarah said. 'I chose this. So shut up.'

*

'Happy Christmas,' a waiter said doubtfully, handing them menus. He was of indeterminate origin but darkly handsome and quite possibly Lebanese, and was wearing a Santa hat.

'Just out of interest,' Richard said to him, 'are you a Christian?'

The man laughed nervously and shied away from their table.

'For God's sake, Richard,' Sarah said. 'You wouldn't ask a white person that.'

He shrugged off her criticism. He was newly cocky, having survived the night of the long knives, the 'purge' as he referred to it. Sarah couldn't imagine how – something underhand, she supposed, some Faustian pact. He had backed the wrong side in the great debate and had been terrified of being flung into the outer darkness. Fear had softened him, made him almost human, but now that he was safe he had reverted to being the old Richard.

Her birthday was just before Christmas, a proximity that irritated her family, as if she had chosen the date herself. As a child they had solved the dilemma by combining her presents: 'This is for your birthday *and* your Christmas, Sally.' Something which had seemed enormously unfair at the time. Now, too.

They had met – so long ago – at university. Sarah and Richard (though she was still Sally then). 'When Dick met Sally,' someone said, as if they were players in a romantic comedy, but really it was neither romantic nor comic. (It was a marriage.)

He had been a posh boy, she had been a poor girl. An old story. No one ever called him Dick except, occasionally, his brother, Robert. He reciprocated by calling his brother Bob. It was a family joke: Dick and Bob. They were furiously competitive. Sarah was surprised they hadn't killed each other.

Both she and Richard had studied law, but she had travelled before university – India, Thailand, Australia, the usual – whereas he had worked at Sotheby's for a year in some kind of front-of-house capacity. Not really what Sarah would have called work. He had never been interested in travel. Two weeks with the children in France in the summer was all he was ever prepared to compromise on. 'Gîte hell,' he called it. He preferred Cornwall. Sarah hated Cornwall, it did nothing but rain.

One day, as they came out of a tedious jurisprudence class in their second term, he turned to her and said 'Fancy a coffee?' and she said 'OK' and that was that, their fates sealed by a couple of bitter cappuccinos in the student bar. Afterwards they went back to the flat he shared with two other posh boys and he put a bootleg copy of Gary Numan's *I, Assassin* on to his tape deck because even then he was pretending to be someone he wasn't.

He had no feeling for music, current or otherwise, and the tape was from the extensive pirated collection belonging to one of the other posh boys, who these days was a music industry mogul and spent a lot of his time harassing Richard about the implementation of the copyright laws, 'which have absolutely nothing to do with me', Richard groused. 'I'm in Education, for Christ's sake.' He had recently moved from Health ('a poisoned chalice if ever there was one'). So she was seduced to Numan intoning 'White Boys And Heroes', which was not what she would have necessarily chosen. Richard saw himself as both, she supposed.

Apart from her father, he was the only person who still called her Sally. When she became a barrister she had reverted to the more earnest-sounding 'Sarah', although she had taken Richard's surname. He had already fought an unwinnable by-election ('taking one for the party') and he needed his new spouse to 'sound like a wife, not a feminist'. ('Sarah Kingshott, Richard's wife, pleased to meet you.') She had laughed and indulged him, but only because her own name was Pratt and she wanted to be a QC eventually, and Kingshott made her sound as though she were halfway there already. ('Sarah Kingshott, QC. How do you do?') She knew that Sally Pratt still dwelt inside her though, waiting to make her move.

'Are you listening to me?' he said, flapping the menu.

'No, sorry, I was miles away.'

'Are you having a starter?' He was a man of appetite.

'No.'

'Well, I am.'

The first time she had taken Richard home to Sheffield (more than a year after those cappuccinos; she had delayed the introduction as long as possible, for her parents' sake rather than his), her mother had greeted her with open arms on the doorstep and shouted over her shoulder, 'Bill! Sally's here!' in a way that was infinitely more effusive than when she had actually lived with her parents. (It had never struck her that they might miss her when she was gone. Youth was callous, she knew that now.)

When she had disentangled herself from her mother's awkward embrace she caught the expression of surprise on Richard's face as he stared down the narrow white-woodchipped hallway of the small semi. She had never really talked about her home and she had no idea what image he had formed in his mind. She supposed he had expected something more gritty and northern, a mean little back-to-back terrace, her mother in headscarf and curlers, her father in a tin bath in front of the fire. The nondescript Fifties ex-council house and her father's member-ship of the local Conservative club must have wrong-footed him. The kitchen, fitted out with new oak laminate cupboards, the ugly stone fireplace and double-glazed windows were all evidence that her parents had come up in the world. Richard had hoped for sedi-tion but instead he found that her mother enjoyed passive evenings in front of the TV, eating crisps and KitKats, while her father downed a modest two pints of Tetley's Bitter and played a game of snooker at the Conservative club.

'He's very good-looking,' her mother said as they washed the pots together after a ham salad and a frozen cheesecake from Marks & Spencer. It wasn't a compliment, more the opposite.

For her part, Sarah had been equally surprised to hear Richard's parents declaring themselves to be 'old-fashioned Liberals'. They were Whigs, really, more Tory than the Tories. Mr Kingshott Senior was a bumbling country squire from another century and Mrs Kingshott was a sovereign figure, as autocratic as a large bird of prey (Sarah was the prey).

The Kingshotts lived in Oxfordshire in

an enormous, rather grubby house called 'the Manor' that looked as though it hadn't been decorated in decades. Dog hair everywhere and the smell of something dead in a downstairs cloakroom that was as big as her parents' living room. 'The filthy rich,' she said to her mother, who would have been horrified by the untidiness and general lack of cleanliness, but her mother never saw 'the Manor' as she died of pancreatic cancer towards the end of Sarah's third year at university.

By the time she graduated Sarah was four months pregnant and had, rather reluctantly, a wedding ring on her finger. The wedding had been modest, the baby and her mother's recent death curtailing the celebration. Would she have married Richard if she hadn't fallen pregnant? Probably not. 'You've made your bed, now you have to lie in it,' her father said, when she was thinking of leaving not long after the baby – Tom – was born. ('It's not you, it's me,' she said to Richard. Which was true. Now it was the opposite.) Her father was a harsh judge of people due to a loveless childhood. His own father had been a steel worker, killed in a horrific accident when he was just a boy. ('Molten steel' was all he would say.)

Richard had begged her to come back, said that he needed her, and she supposed that she was flattered, because everyone admired him in those days. He was the coming man and everyone told her how lucky she was to have him. Nowadays people were more likely to say how lucky he was to have her. 'You just have to knuckle under and get on with it,' her father told her. That was the Pratt family motto: 'Knuckle under and get on with it.' A donkey ambulant on a field of nettles on their coat of arms. So she did. Get on.

Her father was still alive, still listening to Radio 4 and hobbling along to the Conservative club every evening. She visited him more regularly these days. She liked the way it never occurred to him not to speak the truth.

Despite her father's political leanings, Richard used her 'working-class background' to his advantage. Her father had owned an ironmongery shop and Sarah didn't think that qualified as working class, but it did to Richard, of course. He had attended Charterhouse, following in his brother's and father's footsteps. When he was a boy he didn't know anyone who got their hands dirty for a living. Now he was an MP everyone he knew had dirty hands.

While he was doing prep and beating up smaller boys at Charterhouse, Sarah was delivering the evening papers on her bike and working on the cheese counter in Liptons every Saturday.

He used her to mollify his origins. 'My wife is from the north!' he would proclaim on the hustings in the early days, as if she were some kind of Celtic tribal leader (how nice that would be), raising a subdued cheer among the crowd. As a reward for his self-sacrifice (he lost by over twenty thousand votes) he was given the opportunity of a more genteel constituency and he no longer needed to champion her 'industrial' background. He stayed elected because he was a bit of a personality, the big silverback. Often on TV, 'not afraid to give his opinion', 'speaks his mind'. And so on. A showman. Or a wanker, depending on your viewpoint.

They had a house in his rural constituency, although he treated it more as a holiday home really. At the beginning of the marriage they had bought a place in Doughty Street, near where Charles Dickens once lived. (Helped by some family money – his family, it went without saying.) Lovely house, if a bit gloomy, but she could walk to the Temple, where she was in Chambers. Not straight away, of course, she had to fight a bit in those days, northern girl, humble background and so on. She had wanted babies *and* a dazzling career. It had been the Eighties, she was greedy, she wanted it all, like you were supposed to. Now she didn't really want any of it. 'I just wanted *some* of it,' Mandy, Richard's secretary, said to her once, rather sadly.

She had Tom first, then, a few years later, Emma. Both times she went back to work after a week. (How ridiculous that seemed now.) The nanny used to bring Emma to Middle Temple Gardens, where Sarah breastfed her. The fact that they had a nanny was *not* something that was shouted on the hustings.

The children had gone to private schools, a fact that was also eradicated from Richard's history. 'I'm at *Education*, I'm a *socialist*' – well, that was debatable, she thought. 'I can't be seen to have spent a fortune on fees for a private school.'

'I spent the fortune,' she pointed out.

Her own good girls' grammar school (a state school, gone now) had been her ticket out from a life trapped between white-woodchipped walls. It was different for Tom and Emma. Success was the birthright given to them by their parents – Richard Kingshott MP and Sarah Kingshott, QC. A 'power couple', as Sarah had seen them described in a Sunday newspaper magazine supplement. (*'Who are the movers and shakers these days?'* What crap.) There were potted biographies for each of them, histories that made them seem like different people.

'*He*: self-proclaimed people's man, surprisingly scandal-free and not afraid to challenge his party.' (Why 'surprisingly'? she wondered.)

'*She*: lioness of the High Court courts, the woman who defended bullion thief Michael Angers and racist killer Timothy Blair.' (He wasn't a racist, just a killer. She was forever defending herself rather than her clients.)

'*Together*: they have had their own personal struggles, there was a rumour of a separation for a short time in the Nineties and their son narrowly escaped a prison sentence for criminal damage. *He* says his son's problems gave him greater understanding of mental health issues. *She* refuses to comment on the subject.'

He was careful – no overblown expenses or obvious bribes. No holidays taken on some Russian oligarch's yacht. And he had never struck her as the unfaithful type. He was too lazy and she gave him the gloss of legitimacy that he otherwise lacked. When she had been going to leave him after those first few rocky months of marriage he had begged her to stay, had even cried. 'I need you,' he said and she felt sorry for him. 'He did the same to me,' Mandy told her, 'when I was offered the job at Number Ten.' Mandy had been Richard's secretary for years. He probably couldn't function without her, but she was closer to Sarah than she was to him.

'Mum, why don't you just leave Dad?' Emma said. 'You don't love him, you don't even like him any more.' Sarah supposed hypocrisy seemed a crime to a thirty-year-old, not a way of life. Emma and Tom didn't much like Richard either. Somewhere along the line, when Sarah hadn't been looking, Richard had sold his soul to the devil, yet it felt like she was the one paying the ransom.

He produced a little gift-wrapped box and placed it on the table in front of her. 'Happy birthday,' he said again.

A brooch, pretty, a little black cat with tiny emerald eyes. Victorian. Nobody wore brooches any more, except for the Queen, but it was the kind of thing Sarah liked. No doubt Mandy had chosen it. He ran his hand through his hair. It was a gesture he had developed over the years as a signal – 'Get me out of here' usually, or some other sign of dissatisfaction, aimed at either herself or Mandy. He had good hair – almost too good, really.

'You're making that sign,' she said.

She was startled by the appearance of a

waiter, bearing aloft a small cupcake with a candle. The waiter was joined by a handful of other waiters and they all sang 'Happy Birthday' to her in a touchingly cheerful fashion and she suddenly softened towards Richard, but then she realized he was as surprised as she was, so Mandy must have arranged the little cake.

'Make a wish,' he said. So she closed her eyes and blew out the candle and wished.

He had drunk nearly a whole bottle of wine and she had no idea what he might have imbibed beforehand, although his tolerance for alcohol was remarkable. A solid night of drinking that would have felled a younger man left him merely ebullient, and indeed now he was brandishing his car keys and strutting along the pavement like a hero. She hailed a cab and said, 'Don't be an idiot, Richard, you're well over the limit.

Get in.' He fell asleep almost immediately, giving her an opportunity to study his self-satisfied features.

Turned out he was having an affair. She was genuinely surprised (what an idiot she was!) when Mandy said, 'Do you fancy lunch?' and over a corner table in J Sheekey's she showed Sarah the evidence in his texts and his diary. 'She's called Lily,' Mandy said. 'She's half your age and a researcher in the Home Office.' Mandy was ruthless. And fair. And loyal. Just not to Richard.

'I don't want to go all Harry Potter,' Mandy said, 'but I think between us we can do something about him.'

Both Tom and Emma came to the Doughty Street house for Christmas dinner. Tom had a new wife and a new baby. The baby wore a bib that said, 'Baby's First Christmas.'

'Where's Dad?' Tom puzzled. 'Why isn't he here?'

'He's here in spirit,' Sarah said.

'What does that mean, Mum?' Emma frowned.

'It's a bit hard to explain.' She supposed she would have to come up with something, but not now, not at Christmas. The turkey had exhausted her.

'The tree's lovely,' Tom's new wife said. 'I love your decorations. Are they from Liberty's?'

'Some of them,' Sarah said. She went over to the Christmas tree and gazed at one of the baubles. It was made of clear glass and there was a figure inside, a homunculus, a tiny Santa Claus. No one except Sarah noticed that the tiny Santa Claus was jumping up and down in a fury, banging on the inside of the glass sphere. No one could hear him shouting, demanding to be released from his little festive prison. One of the little black cat's emerald eyes winked at him and Sarah murmured, 'Happy Christmas, Richard.' He was going to have to knuckle under and get on with it, wasn't he? Sarah set the bauble spinning, faster and faster, until the tiny Santa Claus was just a blur of red and white.

Small Mercies

The week before Christmas. A light sifting of snow on Gerald's lawn and an unaccustomed chill in his heart. 'Just you and me then, boy,' he said to the Dog. The Dog stared soulfully at him because it was usually about this time of night that Gerald brought out the mince pies.

Gerald had never spent Christmas on his own. The day had always been passed mindlessly in the company of either his mother or his ex-girlfriend, Anthea, and, once (a memory still too awful to dwell on), with both of them together. Anthea (or 'That Woman' as both his mother and the Dog thought of her) was gone now, of course, married to an accountant and living unhappily ever afterwards in Surrey.

Sometimes, Gerald wondered what would have happened if he and Anthea had lasted, had stumbled all the way to the altar — would he even now be surreptitiously filling stockings at the ends of small beds and drinking Santa's sherry while Anthea wrapped presents in front of a Yuletide log burning in the hearth? And, yes, Gerald did understand that this was a ridiculously utopian vision of Christmas. But some of it might have been true. The sherry anyway.

These imaginary children would have called him Dad, wouldn't they? No one had ever called him Dad, and he suspected no one ever would now. The thought made Gerald's spirits droop even further.

The Dog wagged its tail encouragingly. It sensed the mince pies slipping away.

'You'll be all right on your own for Christmas, won't you, Gerald?' his mother had said, rather indifferently and rather late in the day, as she packed her suitcase – an unseasonable trove of suntan cream, beach towels, diarrhoea tablets and an extraordinary piece of industrial-strength corsetry that Gerald could only presume was a swimming costume.

His mother – who had previously considered a week's holiday in Eastbourne an extravagance – was off on a three-week cruise around 'the Med' in the company of her giddy new cohorts.

Several months ago, his mother had moved into a 'retirement complex'. Gerald, previously unacquainted with such places, had feared it would be a dismal, God's-waiting-room kind of place, full of shuffling ancients zimmering their way through their twilight years. 'If I ever get like that,' his mother said crossly, 'then I hope you'll ask a vet to put me down.' It was some time before Gerald could shake off a disturbing mental picture of sitting in the vet's waiting room with his mother in an oversize cat-basket, awaiting a final, fatal dose of Immobilon.

Gerald wondered how he *would* feel when his mother shuffled off her mortal coil – hopefully in the antiseptic environment of a hospital rather than a veterinary surgery. He imagined her, pain-free and comfortable, exhibiting unusual acceptance ('Everyone has to go some time, Gerald'), before passing peacefully with a beatific smile on her face. It seemed unlikely – his mother was not the beatific kind and he doubted that she would arrive at the pearly gates without a list of complaints ready in her hand before she'd even seen what lay beyond. Thinking about his mother's death, Gerald was (mildly) ashamed that the only feeling it gave rise to was one of relief, whereas if he allowed himself to imagine the Dog's demise, a hot, hard stone of grief lodged itself beneath his breastbone. 'Gerald? Gerald, are you all right?' his mother asked sharply.

Gerald soon discovered that he could not have been more mistaken in his prejudices about the retirement complex. Never had he encountered such a busy bunch of people as his mother's neighbours. They swam and jogged and golfed, they played bridge and Scrabble, they organized tea-dances, investment clubs and reading groups. They held endless coffee mornings and afternoon teas and threw parties at the drop of a hat. 'The grey pound,' his mother said mysteriously.

Gerald thought it a great shame that all this social whirling was restricted to people of pensionable age – it was exactly the kind of life that would have benefited middle-aged bachelors. 'Well, it won't be too long before you *are* old, Gerald,' his mother said carelessly. (Yes, but *you* will always be older, he thought and chastised himself for his lack of charity.) 'Our first port of call is Marseilles,' she said as nonchalantly as an old sea dog. 'I'll send you a postcard from there, you're not to worry about me.' (It would be nice, he thought, if for once she would worry about *him*.) 'Anyway,' she continued blithely, 'you can spend Christmas with your friend Colin. He hasn't got anyone now either.'

'Thanks,' Gerald said.

*

On his way out, Gerald passed through the communal lounge, festooned with decorations and home to a huge, brightly lit Christmas tree. A lively poker game was in progress. 'Deal you in, Gerald?' someone offered. Gerald declined, indicating his wristwatch as if he could not afford the time for such pleasurable idleness. 'You wait until you're retired,' one of the poker-players laughed, 'you'll wonder how you ever had time to work.'

Hurrying out into the dark night, Gerald felt a sudden craving for a shoulder to lean on and made his way to the Lamb and Flag, where, since his divorce, Colin had taken up residence in the snug bar. Colin and Gerald had known each other since primary school, a shared history which seemed to overcome the fact that they had nothing else in common. 'Here's to life's losers,' Colin said cheerfully, raising his pint glass and toasting Gerald. 'Plus,' he added, 'no trouble and strife to spoil the big day, Gerald. We'll be as free as birds. We can start drinking at breakfast,' he continued enthusiastically, 'and carry on until we're unconscious.'

Christmas Eve. 'Ho, ho, ho,' Gerald said mirthlessly, pouring himself a large malt whisky in the kitchen. He carried it, along with a plate of mince pies, through to the living room. The Dog pattered after him. 'Living my best life,' Gerald said sardonically to it as it jumped on the sofa next to him. The Dog always sat on the left, Gerald on the right. Gerald also slept on the right-hand side of his bed and had woken on more than one occasion to find the Dog lying next to him, its head on the pillow. When the Dog was a puppy, Gerald had followed the advice to leave him to sleep in a basket down in the kitchen, but the tiny whimpering noises that had carried on throughout the night had been too much for him and since then the Dog had shared the bedroom with Gerald.

Gerald drank the whisky rather quickly, like medicine, and considered a second one. It was Christmas, after all. The living room, free of any Christmas decorations apart from a half-hearted attempt on Gerald's part to display his (rather meagre) trawl of Christmas cards, looked cheerless.

'What's it all about?' he asked the Dog, ruffling its fur absent-mindedly. 'What's the point of it all? Redundant,' Gerald continued gloomily. 'Surplus to requirements. That's me.'

On the day that Gerald's mother had sailed off into the sunshine, Gerald had turned up at work as usual, nothing much on his mind other than whether he might manage to manoeuvre Jill Stewart from Sales and Marketing under the mistletoe at the office party, and he had been called into Rodney Leyland's office. Rodney Leyland was Gerald's line manager and it seemed painfully ironic that he was currently dressed as Santa Claus. 'Kids' party,' he explained, pulling off his beard.

'Ho, ho, ho,' Gerald said, entering into the festive spirit.

'Gerald,' Rodney Leyland said gently, 'we need to have a chat.'

'Downsizing,' Gerald explained mournfully to the Dog. 'They're calling it "early retirement" to make it sound better, but frankly that makes it worse. I've made not much over a half-century and I've already been bowled out. On the scrap heap.' The Dog listened with its head cocked in a way that suggested sympathy although actually its mind had wandered to the last uneaten mince pies.

Gerald felt guilty; he did not normally indulge in fits of melancholy. There were so many people in the world – most people, in fact, if he thought about it – who were worse off than himself that Gerald tried always to be grateful for what he had, to be thankful for the small mercies that life sent his way. And yet tonight, Gerald felt as if he had nothing.

'I mean, it's not the money, they've given me pretty good severance pay. It's just . . . no one wants me.' The Dog pushed its wet, cold nose into Gerald's hand and wagged its tail in an effort to prove the contrary.

'Of course, you need a walk, old boy. I'm sorry.' Gerald made an effort to rouse himself from the torpor he'd fallen into. Self-pity wasn't something he wanted to reveal to anyone, even the Dog. Especially the Dog.

Gerald tossed the last mince pie whole into his mouth and the Dog watched its trajectory with hopeless despair.

'Let's go,' Gerald said.

The Dog trotted ahead, oblivious to the cold. Gerald followed at a somewhat less eager pace. Gerald's house was at the edge of the suburbs, on the border between town and country, a landscape which Gerald found rather uninspiring and which the Dog found almost unbearably exciting.

Their first stop, for they were both creatures of habit, was the river. Gerald, as usual, stayed on the bridge while the Dog snuffled and truffled down on the bank. The cold snap had already transformed the water into a slurry of ice. Gerald leant on the parapet, lost in thought. Would it really make any difference, he wondered, if he slipped down into those chilly waters, never to resurface again? Had his life ever made a difference to anyone? The world would surely go on just the same if he had never been born. Such thoughts were new to Gerald and he was surprised – and rather alarmed – to discover how easily they came to him. An image came suddenly to Gerald's mind – an image of this very same river, on a hot, still day nearly forty years ago. And Colin – as pale and podgy then as he was now – thrashing around helplessly in the middle of the river, calling in a desperate voice for Gerald to save him. If he'd stopped to think about it, Gerald – a poor swimmer – might not have dived in, might not have hauled the dead weight of Colin to the bank, but he didn't think – for once in his life – he simply jumped.

'Owe you one, Gerald,' was Colin's habitual toast in the Lamb and Flag, and he didn't mean a round.

The Dog scrambled back up to the road and signalled it was ready to move on with a short bark. Gerald, proficient in dog language, left the bridge and set off obediently.

The road took them past the local church and Gerald was puzzled for a moment at the sight of lights blazing and the sound of reedy voices reaching for the descant of 'Oh, Come, All Ye Faithful' until he realized it was the Midnight Service, long since abandoned as a ritual by Gerald. In fact, Gerald had not been inside this church, or any other, since his brother's funeral. Gerald's brother, David – a golden boy and his mother's clear favourite – had been killed in a car accident on the eve of his twenty-first birthday. Gerald had been about to embark on a degree in languages – a springboard, he'd hoped, to an exotic and interesting future. After his brother's death, however, his mother retreated into a profound depression, and, in an effort to comfort her, Gerald had elected to postpone university and take a temporary humdrum job with a local company.

Eventually, his mother came to terms with her loss, but by then it seemed too late for Gerald's exotic and interesting future, and anyway by then 'humdrum' had become a way of life for Gerald. These days the occasional 'Banquet for Two' at the Lucky Dragon was the nearest Gerald got to exotic – and when the person you were sharing with was Colin, that wasn't really the right word.

Gerald wondered if his mother would have grieved so much for him as she had for David. He doubted it.

People spilled out of the church, their happy voices ringing as cheerfully as bells on the cold air. The Dog wagged its tail, ready to exchange seasonal greetings, but Gerald walked away briskly, calling on the Dog to follow him. He didn't think he could handle all that Christmas cheer.

David had been an attractive extrovert, drawing people into his orbit without having to make any effort. Gerald had lived in the long shadow he cast. At parties, David was the centre of attention while Gerald was the one in the corner, talking to the bore no one else would listen to – or, more likely, the one clearing the dirty glasses and ministering to the person being sick in the bathroom. That was how he had met Anthea, dizzy with drink at some party that Gerald had attended reluctantly. He had helped her home in a very gentlemanly fashion and she had called him a life-saver. Anthea had just come out of a bad relationship, drinking too much, partying too much, and Gerald had been a sobering influence in all ways. 'You're a rock, Gerald,' she'd once said gratefully, 'You got me back on my feet,' but it was a gratitude that soon dissipated. Once back on those feet – in three-inch Jimmy Choo heels – she walked off without a backward glance.

'You know,' Gerald said as they turned a bend in the road and started heading for home, 'we're probably lucky that Anthea left. She wasn't exactly easy to please, was she?' The Dog stifled a growl and kept its own counsel.

'And now I'm free.' Gerald frowned,

pausing on the garden path to contemplate the novelty of this idea. There really was nothing to stop him having an interesting life if he chose. He had a sudden vision of himself and the Dog striding through a countryside dusty with sun, or drinking Chianti (Gerald, not the Dog) against a golden backdrop of sunflowers, or perhaps driving along avenues of cypresses in a neatly fitted-out camper van. 'Free as a bird,' Gerald murmured and laughed, much to the Dog's surprise.

'A camper van,' he said to the Dog. The Dog, to its credit, managed to look thoughtful. 'And the open road. What do you think?'

The phone was ringing as Gerald turned the key in the lock, and when he picked it up his mother's not very maternal tones were wishing him 'Happy Christmas'. She was vague about where she was – 'Italy, maybe' – and sounded quite tipsy. There was the noise of shipboard merriment in the background and it was difficult to make out his mother's words, laced as they were with emotion and free alcohol.

'I can't hear you,' Gerald said. He could hear her perfectly well, but he wanted the satisfaction of making his mother bellow the words down the phone.

'I love you, Gerald,' she shouted, so loudly that even the Dog on the other side of the room heard her. They pantomimed astonishment at each other.

'Merry Christmas,' Colin said, raising his glass.

Christmas dinner was a 'Banquet for Two' brought home from the Lucky Dragon, accompanied by a bottle of champagne that had been lurking in the bottom of Gerald's fridge. Colin had contributed a couple of Christmas crackers left over from when he had a wife.

'I owe you one,' Colin said, draining his glass and pouring another.

'You do,' Gerald agreed cheerfully. He raised his own glass and made a toast. 'To small mercies,' he said.

'Oh, yeah, those too,' Colin agreed, spooning sticky rice into his mouth.

And the Dog, in prime position on the hearthrug, where it was gnawing a particularly meaty Christmas bone, glanced at Gerald and thought, It's a wonderful life.

KATE ATKINSON

BEHIND THE SCENES AT THE MUSEUM

A surprising, tragicomic and subversive family saga set in York, Kate Atkinson's prizewinning first novel, like all her novels, has a mystery at its heart.

'Little short of a masterpiece.'
Daily Mail

HUMAN CROQUET

A multilayered, moving novel about the forest of Arden, a girl who drops in and out of time, and the heartrending mystery of a lost mother.

'Brilliant and engrossing.'
Penelope Fitzgerald

EMOTIONALLY WEIRD

Set in Dundee, this clever, comic novel depicts student life in all its wild chaos, and a girl's poignant quest for her father.

'Achingly funny . . . executed with wit and mischief.'
Meera Syal

NOT THE END OF THE WORLD
Kate Atkinson's first collection of short stories –
playful and profound.

'Moving and funny, and crammed with incidental wisdom.'
Sunday Times

LIFE AFTER LIFE
What if you had the chance to live your life again and
again, until you finally got it right?

'Grips the reader's imagination on the first page and never
lets go. If you wish to be moved and astonished, read it.'
Hilary Mantel

A GOD IN RUINS
For all Teddy – would-be-poet, RAF bomber pilot, husband and
father – endures in battle, his greatest challenge will be to face
living in a future he never expected to have.

'Kate Atkinson's finest work, and confirmation that her
genre-defying writing continues to surprise and dazzle.'
Observer

TRANSCRIPTION
In 1940, 18-year-old Juliet is reluctantly recruited into the
world of espionage: in 1950, working at the BBC, she is
confronted by figures from her past.

'Reminds you how deeply satisfying
good fiction can be.'
Sunday Telegraph

Featuring Jackson Brodie

CASE HISTORIES
The first novel to feature Jackson Brodie, the former police detective, who finds himself investigating three separate cold murder cases in Cambridge, while haunted by a tragedy in his own past.

'The best mystery of the decade.'
Stephen King

ONE GOOD TURN
Jackson Brodie, in Edinburgh during the Festival, is drawn into a vortex of crimes and mysteries, each containing a kernel of the next, like a set of nesting Russian dolls.

'The most fun I've had with a novel this year.'
Ian Rankin

WHEN WILL THERE BE GOOD NEWS?
A six-year-old girl witnesses an appalling crime. Thirty years later, Jackson Brodie is on a fatal journey that will hurtle him into its aftermath.

'Effortlessly bridges the gap between commercial and literary fiction.'
Fay Weldon

STARTED EARLY, TOOK MY DOG

Jackson Brodie returns to Yorkshire in search of his roots while shopping mall security chief Tracy Waterhouse makes an impulse purchase that will turn her life upside down.

'The best British novel of the year.'
Heat

BIG SKY

In a quiet seaside village in Yorkshire, an encounter with a desperate man on a crumbling cliff leads Jackson Brodie to a sinister network.

'A masterclass in what can be done with crime fiction.'
Sunday Times

BIG SKY
KATE ATKINSON

Jackson Brodie has relocated to a quiet seaside
village in North Yorkshire, in the occasional
company of his recalcitrant teenage son Nathan
and ageing Labrador Dido, both at the discretion
of his former partner Julia. It's a picturesque
setting, but there's something darker lurking
behind the scenes.

Jackson's current job, gathering proof of an
unfaithful husband for a suspicious wife, seems
straightforward, but a chance encounter with
a desperate man on a crumbling cliff leads him
across a sinister network – and back into the path
of his old friend Reggie.

Old secrets and new lies intersect in this
breathtaking new novel, both sharply funny
and achingly sad, by one of the most dazzling
and surprising writers at work today.

Reading is one of life's simplest pleasures. But what if you were losing your sight to cataracts, or for lack of a pair of glasses?

Sightsavers' vision is of a world where no one is blind from avoidable causes and where people with disabilities participate equally in society. We are an international organization working with partners to save the sight of some of the world's most vulnerable people, treating conditions like cataracts and providing glasses to people who need them. We campaign for disability rights, and are getting close to achieving a milestone in human health, as we fight to eliminate debilitating diseases that affect more than a billion people.

To find out more, or to donate, visit sightsavers.org.

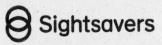 Sightsavers